MICKEY MOUSE MOVIE STORIES

Story and Illustrations by Staff of Walt Disney Studio
Introduction by Maurice Sendak

Harry N. Abrams, Inc., Publishers, New York

Project Director: Darlene Geis

Library of Congress Cataloging-in-Publication Data

Mickey Mouse movie stories / story and illustrations
by staff of Walt Disney Studio.
       p.   cm.
    Summary: Presents several adventures of Mickey Mouse,
Minnie Mouse, and Pluto illustrated with drawings
from animated films made in the Disney Studios
during the 1930's.
    ISBN 0-8109-1529-4
    1. Mickey Mouse (Cartoon character)—Juvenile fiction.
[1. Mickey Mouse (Cartoon character)—Fiction. 2. Mice—Fiction.
3. Motion picture cartoons.] I. Walt Disney Productions.
PZ7.M58195 1988
[Fic]—dc 19
                                                    88-3503
                                                    CIP

Copyright © 1934 The Walt Disney Company
Introduction copyright © 1988 Harry N. Abrams, Inc.

A Times Mirror Company

Printed and bound in Japan

INTRODUCTION

The Mickey who appears in this best-of-all Mickey books is the one and only "real" Mickey, that elegantly fashioned mouse of the mid-thirties I fell fast in love with years ago and for whose sake I have spent a good deal of my adult life recollecting and collecting.

When *Mickey Mouse Movie Stories* was originally published in 1934 Mickey and I were only six years old. Even then I begrudged my idol nothing, certainly not his instant and stunning success. He deserved it all.

Just five months after my laborious breech birth in June 1928 Mickey had smoothly and triumphantly burst on the scene at New York's Colony Theatre starring in *Steamboat Willie*. Despite my lead Mickey was already far ahead. In the natural way of humankind, I staggered from one psychosexual stage to another as Mickey zoomed undaunted, unencumbered, and even Freud-less, to the top. But unlike the siblings I was heir to, the Mouse was never my rival. His obvious physical superiority and charismatic success were more than compensated for by the great joy he gave me.

Mickey's infancy flashed by so speedily that I completely missed his original rat-faced-black-hand-and-foot look. By the time my common consciousness focused on his uncommon beauty he was round and radiant, all gloved and shoed, looking just the way he does in these pages.

By coincidence two of the movie cartoons whose stories are retold here played a significant role in my early life. *Gulliver Mickey,* published as the storybook, *Mickey Mouse in Pygmyland* in 1936, was the first book given to me by my doting older sister. I literally treasured it to death. With all due respect to the film version, the book's virtues were unique. It was printed on cheap, wonderful-smelling yellow pulp paper, illustrated with richly black, blurred, and over-inked pictures.

Mickey Mouse the Mail Pilot (listed herein as "The Mail Pilot") was a vintage example of that glorious and now defunct form of publishing: the delicious, fat "Big Little Book." It ran to an obese 320 pages. Like its fellow volumes it was of a size and shape that invited the reader to fondle, sniff, chew and perhaps read. All of which I did. These books measured 3½ x 4½″ and had fabulous full-color cardboard covers. The story and pictures were also printed on that irresistible aromatic pulp. What most enthralled me about *Mickey Mouse the Mail Pilot* was the picture on the front cover of Mickey in his airplane: a magnificently utilitarian vehicle that bent and twisted with dough-like pliancy to suit the needs of the intrepid pilot. I had to have that red and yellow airplane! Thirty-seven years later I gratified that implacable childhood wish by placing my hero, Mickey, in his, and my, own dough plane on the front cover of my picture book *In the Night Kitchen*. This book encapsulated my passion for Mickey, movies, New York City, and the strange, dark, doomy Thirties that, for me, were lit only by Mickey's bright, beaming smile on the screen, a smile that caused me to scream joyfully with Pavlovian regularity in those lovely Temples of Art: the movie houses that lined 18th Avenue in Brooklyn of olden days.

Now that I am old enough to treasure the mysteries of my childhood I realize that Mickey plays a small but significant part. He turns up regularly in cheerful dreams and I have written a great deal about him, conjuring his graphic image in an effort to make an aesthetic case for my admittedly feverish affection. While I uncover bits of truth in these accounts, what strikes me is the unwavering trust I had in him then, a trust that still, amazingly, resides in me now.

Private musings and nostalgic associations aside, *Mickey Mouse Movie Stories* is a special favorite on a more objective level. It is perhaps, with Book 1, the prettiest book Disney Studio and McKay ever produced. The liveliness and dazzling invention of the early Disney artists and the quality of the black and white are still simply ravishing.

Mickey and I are sixty years old this year and, along with our common initial, we have shared a common fate; we are both working artists, entertainers who aim to please. I would like to think that I have finally caught up with my fantasy sibling. But then I turn these pages and see him captured forever in all his youth and freshness. I should look so good.

Maurice Sendak

MICKEY MOUSE

MOVIE STORIES

MICKEY MOUSE MOVIE STORIES

Story and Illustrations by Staff of Walt Disney Studio

Introduction by Maurice Sendak

Harry N. Abrams, Inc., Publishers, New York

CONTENTS

MICKEY'S GOOD DEED

*I*t was Christmas Eve. Sleighs full of holiday merry-makers jingled up and down the street, and last-minute shoppers were hurrying home through the snow, laden with bundles. Some of them paused a moment and listened to Christmas Carols played by a tattered little figure on a street corner. Beside him, a big dog howled a lusty accompaniment.

Mickey Mouse glanced down at a battered tin cup on the ground beside him. It contained three washers, two buttons and an old rusty bolt! Penniless, cold and hungry, he put the cup in his pocket and sloshed up the street through the snow. His way led past a restaurant and he looked inside hungrily. Pluto put his paws up on the window and licked the glass. He was SO close to the food inside—but he couldn't even smell it! He turned away sadly and followed his master.

Passing a large house they paused and looked in the windows. There on the floor was a rich but badly spoiled youngster, surrounded by toys and wanting none of them. Every time his father or the butler would hand him a new toy, the youngster would shout: "I don't WANT it!" and smash it to the floor.

Then the youngster looked out the window and saw Pluto. He pointed to him and shouted at the top of his lungs: "I want doggie! I want doggie! WAW-W-W-W! I want DOG-GIE!"

The father, willing to do anything to stop his son's crying, said to the butler: "Get that dog for Adelbert. Understand? I don't care what it costs—but GET him!"

Mickey saw the butler come rushing out of the house, shouting: "Say, my man! Look here! Just a moment! I say! Don't go off! I want to buy your dog!"

Mickey decided that the best place for him and Pluto was somewhere else, and off he started as fast as his legs would carry him. As he ran

he looked back over his shoulder and cried: "No! I won't sell him! I won't sell him, I tell you!"

Trying to get away from the butler, Mickey did not see a sleigh coming down the street until it was almost upon him. Both he and Pluto jumped to safety but in the excitement Mickey dropped his cello. He turned around just in time to see it broken and crushed under the runners of the sleigh.

Poor Mickey! This left him with no way of earning money! It seemed as if the whole world were going to have a merry Christmas— everybody but Pluto and himself.

Not caring where they went, the pair wandered across the railroad tracks and stopped in front of a weather-beaten shack that was lighted by a single candle. Mickey peeked through the window, wondering what kind of Christmas the people inside were planning. What he saw made him gasp with amazement. The house and furniture were almost falling to pieces. The cupboard had been bare a long time,

for there were cobwebs in it. There was not even so much as a crust of bread in the room. Such a picture of poverty he had never seen. But the greatest shock came when he looked at the fireplace. On the mantelpiece were hung nine stockings. Nine old, worn-out, tattered stockings hung there with a prayer that Santa Claus would bring their owners a little food and a few toys.

Mickey's eyes filled with tears. He looked at the ragged children, asleep in bed.

"Poor little kids!" he said, half aloud. "And to think I was kickin' about MY hard luck! Gee! If I had a lot o' money, it'd sure be fun t' sneak in there with a whole bag full o' food an' stuff for 'em! But—" He blinked rapidly and wiped away a tear with the back of his hand. "No such luck. If there was only some way I could get a lot o' money—!" Then he stopped and looked at his dog.

"Pluto!" he cried. "There IS a way to get money! That butler said he wanted to buy you!"

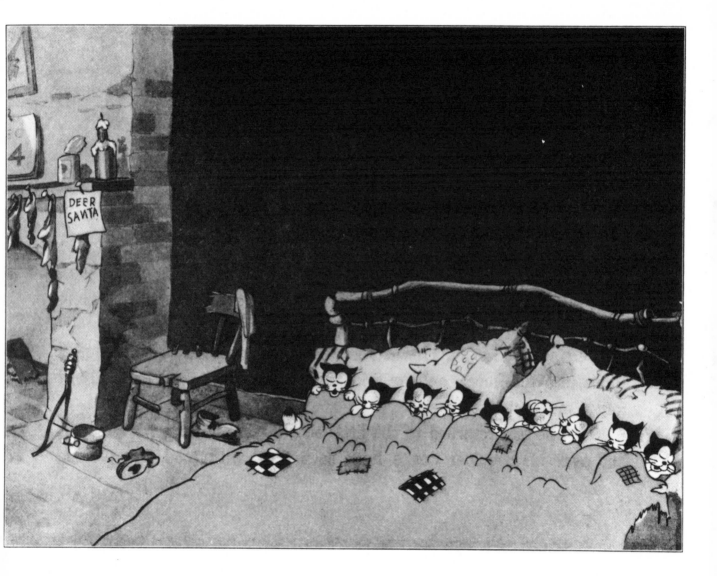

Pluto looked at his master and wagged his tail. Mickey knelt down in the snow and threw his arms around the dog's neck.

"Ol' feller," he sobbed, "there's just nothin' else t' do. It'll give you a good home, where you'll never get hungry. An' it'll give those poor kids a swell Christmas! O' course, I—I hate t' lose you, but there's nine of them an' only one of me! An' if I can make nine kids happy, I guess I'm doin' my bit!"

He wiped away the tears and started back, dragging Pluto with him. When the butler answered his ring, Mickey said: "I'll sell him to you, Mister—if you'll give him a good home."

Putting a roll of bills in his pocket, Mickey watched the butler take Pluto into the house, and he said softly: "Good-bye, ol' pal! Don't forget me—not—not ever!"

Soon he had returned to the little shack. His pockets were empty, but over his shoulder was a huge sack filled with food and bulging

with toys. He wore a little red and white hat and on his face was a long, flowing Santa Claus beard.

Softly opening the door and slipping across the room to the fireplace, he opened the sack. And what a time he had, filling each stocking to the very brim! Around the hearth he put toys of every kind— mechanical toys, dolls, electric trains, wagons, games and musical instruments. Candy canes were distributed all over the room. The cupboard was filled to overflowing with food enough to last the poor family a month or more. And on the table he put a huge turkey, all roasted and ready to eat, together with everything else that makes a perfect Christmas dinner.

When he was through, Mickey looked over at the bed. The children were peacefully sleeping and Mickey smiled happily as he thought what a grand surprise they would get when they awoke the next morning.

As he turned to leave the house, Mickey tripped on a pair of roller skates and in trying to catch himself he kicked a little toy duck. It

went rolling across the room, its head bobbing backward and forward, making a terrific noise: "QUACK! QUACK! QUA-A-A-ACK! QUACK! QUACK! QUA-A-A-ACK!"

Mickey darted for the door. He made it just in time, for no sooner had he rushed through it than he heard loud shouts and shrieks of joy inside the house. The quacking duck had awakened the children.

Mickey sneaked around to the window and looked inside. Never had he seen so much excitement. The children were all over the room at once, some of them eating candy, others playing with their new toys, others emptying their stockings onto the floor, and still others standing around, looking as though they couldn't believe their eyes.

As Mickey turned away from the window his heart was almost bursting. It was a cold night, yet he was warm. He was hungry, yet it didn't bother him. He was still thinking of those children. He had

given them happiness. And happiness is a perfume you can't pour on others without spilling some on yourself.

Wandering through town, Mickey passed few people. Everyone else was in bed. It seemed as though Mickey were the only one that had no home—no place to go.

At last he came to the edge of town and climbed up a little hill. He built a tiny fire and sat down beside it. From his pocket he pulled a lone frankfurter—the only thing to eat he had saved for himself. Poor, forlorn little Mickey! No money, no Christmas dinner, no home and, worst of all, no dog!

And what of Pluto all this time? Once inside the big house he found the youngster was not only spoiled but also cruel. He pestered Pluto, threw things at him, and finally tied a huge turkey to the dog's tail. Pluto tried to get it off, and ran around the room, yowling at the top of his voice, until the butler grabbed him in his arms and threw him out in the snow, shouting: "Get out—and stay out!"

Pluto's first thought was to find Mickey. Sniffing the snow, he finally picked up his master's trail, and away he went, dragging the turkey behind him.

After a long time he found Mickey sitting by the fire. And what a reunion it was! Side by side they sat, eating the turkey until every last morsel was gone. Then they curled up in the snow and went to sleep, keeping each other warm.

Life was good after all. Mickey had made the nine poor children happy and in doing so he had made himself the happiest of all. To this day he says that that was the Merriest Christmas he ever had.

THE MAIL PILOT

The airport was buzzing with activity. A huge armored truck whizzed through the gates and skidded to a stop. From it was lifted a chest of gold which was placed in the mail compartment of a trim little plane. The guards then stood at attention as Pilot Mickey Mouse approached. Mickey returned the salute, quickly checked over his plane, tightened a bolt here, squirted a few drops of oil there, and climbed into the cockpit. From there he squirted a few more shots of oil down over a poster which read: $5000 Reward, Dead or Alive, for the Capture of Pete, the Mail Bandit!" He threw the oil can away and, laughing gaily, he waved at the assembled crowd. Then sput! sputter! fffffffffft! BANG! Whisssssssshhhhhhh! and away he went, zooming into the sky.

Seeing a mass of dark clouds ahead, Mickey smiled grimly.

"Looks like tough weather," he said, half aloud. "But the mail must go through!" And he plunged into the clouds.

As the rain started, Mickey scrunched down into the cockpit as far as he could. The rain poured down over him, but as usual he was prepared, and he reached up and clicked on a pair of tiny windshield wipers mounted on his goggles.

Dodging flashes of lightning, skimming over mountain peaks, plowing through walls of raindrops, Mickey kept forging ahead. Then the snow started falling. It piled up on his wings, almost clogging the propeller, and a film of ice formed over the plane. The motor chugged and puffed and sputtered. The ice and snow were getting too heavy. Unless he could get out of the storm, Mickey knew he would crash against the steep mountains. But he gritted his teeth, stuck out his chin and kept on, repeating over and over again: "The mail must go through!"

Suddenly Mickey's plane roared out of the dark clouds into thinner, whiter ones, and then out into broad sunlight. It was as though Nature

admired the lad's courage and was doing all it could to help him get the mail through.

But Pete, the Mail Bandit, had no such kindly thought. Hiding behind a mountain peak he watched Mickey's plane skimming along, drying out under the soft rays of the sun. Pete started his motor and swooped out to meet the oncoming mail plane.

Mickey was singing happily as he flew along. The storm was over. There was nothing to worry about. The world was a pretty fine place. And then—the bandit struck! His machine gun was trained on Mickey, and he shouted: "HANDS UP!" Mickey obeyed. There was nothing else to do. But as he raised his hands his head was working and so were his feet. He shoved one knee against the joy stick and the plane shot down directly under Pete's, in a steep nose dive.

Pete cursed angrily, and followed Mickey, his machine gun spitting a deadly stream of tracer bullets. Occasionally one cut through the fuselage or zipped through the air close by Mickey's head. Then the

firing stopped. Mickey looked back over his shoulder, thinking he had outdistanced the bandit. But what he saw made his hair stand on end. Pete was close behind and gaining rapidly. He was holding his fire until he got so close he couldn't miss. Mickey scrunched down in the cockpit, knowing the end was close at hand. Pete sighted along the barrel of his machine gun and pulled the trigger.

RAT-A-TAT-A-TAT-A-TAT! Away went one of Mickey's wings. Another burst of fire, and the second wing dropped off. Pete roared with laughter. The bullets were zipping directly above Mickey's plane, so Pete lowered the muzzle slowly and ripped his bullets through Mickey's propeller, finally shooting it away too. Mickey's plane hesitated a second, then turned nose downward.

Down! Down! Down! Spinning dizzily and crazily, Mickey fell toward the earth. Pete followed like a hawk, his evil face contorted in a triumphant leer.

But again Pete failed to count on Mickey's quick-thinking. As his

plane whirled toward the ground Mickey saw a large windmill spinning in the breeze. He headed his plane toward it, and by an almost super-human effort he guided the propeller shaft directly into the center of the windmill.

ZOOM! CRASH! WHIR-R-R-R! The windmill fitted the propeller shaft. It began to spin, faster, faster, faster. Taking a desperate chance, Mickey nosed his plane down and just as he was about to crash he pulled back on the joy stick. The plane leveled off, close to the ground. Then, with the makeshift propeller taking hold, it zoomed upward again.

Cursing harder than ever, Pete followed close behind. He drew a large harpoon out of the cockpit, mounted it on his plane and let fire. It was a bull's-eye! The harpoon stuck into the tail of Mickey's faltering plane and Pete began to haul it back, hand over hand. He knew it was but a matter of time until he had Mickey and the cargo of gold in his hands.

But Mickey had other ideas.   Not far away he saw a church steeple in which were hanging a number of bells, so he headed for it at full speed.   He knew that the bandit would show him no mercy. It would be better to die trying to escape than to fall into Pete's hands.   And there was a chance—a bare chance—that he might get away.

He glanced down at his plane, at the sheared-off wings.   He looked again at the steeple, now near at hand.   With his wings gone, he might be able to fly through the belfry while Pete's plane, dragging along behind, would be shattered.

Closer, closer, closer he came.   Now was the time!   He banked just enough to clear the framework and sailed through the steeple out into the open.   And then—

C-R-R-R-RASH-H-H-H!

Pete's plane flew into a million splinters as it tore through the belfry. Pete himself came flying out the other side, hanging onto the harpoon

rope.   Around his neck was a long string of bells, ringing and dinging and donging merrily as if celebrating Mickey's victory.

Mickey turned around and laughed.   He knew he had won the battle. More than that, he had won it with all the odds against him.   Unarmed and seemingly helpless against the most ruthless mail bandit of all time, Mickey had come out on top, and he was very pleased with his work.

But he knew his job was not yet finished.   He still had to deliver his cargo of gold, and that was no easy task, with his plane disabled as it was, and with Pete sailing along behind like the tail of a kite.

However, the airport was only a few miles away and soon it came in sight..   Mickey approached it slowly and carefully, circling it once or twice, then dropping down directly in the center.   Pete hit the ground right behind Mickey and skidded along for a few feet and then started rolling.   Mickey reached out quickly and cut the rope.   Two aviators saw Pete rolling toward them so they got a mail sack, held it open until

Pete rolled into it, and then tied it up and snapped a padlock on the opening.

The gold was delivered and the mail bandit was captured!

The pilots and mechanics around the airport hoisted Mickey to their shoulders and marched down the field, singing and shouting at the tops of their voices. For Mickey had brought glory to the mail service, and he had nobly upheld their slogan: "The Mail Must Go Through!"

"THE KLONDIKE KID"

A forlorn little figure pulled her shawl higher over her head and leaned against the wind as she fought her way through the driving snow to a window in the Klondike Dance Hall. She pressed her little nose against the pane and looked inside.

There she saw a scene of wild activity. Dozens of hardy miners and husky lumberjacks were singing and dancing and leaning against the long mahogany bar. In one corner of the dance hall Mickey Mouse was sitting on an empty barrel, pounding gay melodies out of a battered old piano. He was having a grand time, laughing, singing and playing as only Mickey can play.

But suddenly he looked up and saw the poor little figure at the window. He got just a glimpse of her before she slumped down exhausted in the snow.

As he opened the window and leaned out to get her, a terrific gust of wind and snow almost blinded him. But he managed to pick her up and carry her across the room, where he seated her on a small barrel by the stove. Lifting the shawl away from her face, he saw that she was crying. He also saw that she was a very, very pretty young girl.

"Hello," he said, smiling. "Who are you?"

"Nobody!" she replied, trying to hold back the tears.

"Haven't ya got any folks?" he asked.

"N-n-nobody!" was the tearful answer.

"Just an orphan?"

"Yes. I'm—I'm—just an orphan."

Mickey laughed. "Me, too! I guess we're both nobodies!"

Minnie joined in his laugh. The tears were nearly gone now, so Mickey took out a big bandana handkerchief and held it up to her nose. "Blow hard!" he said, and she did.

"Are ya hungry?" he asked, and when she nodded he went to get her a bowl of hot soup. But hardly had he returned when the door flew open and in stepped Pierre, the Terror of the Northwest, with both guns blazing.

Mickey was holding the soup up to Minnie's mouth when Pierre spied them. Flashing one of the pistols in their direction, he shot the bowl right out of Mickey's hand.

"Hey!" Mickey cried, startled. "What's the big idea?"

With a wild roar, Pierre leaped at Mickey, swung him around with one hand, and threw him clear across the room. With his other hand Pierre threw a knife which pierced Mickey's pants and pinned him against the wall. Then he lifted Minnie up and held her close to his cruel face.

"Maybe you don' like Pierre! Yes?" he taunted.

"No!" she screamed, and slapped him as hard as she could. But he only put back his head and roared with laughter.

Pierre glanced about the room. It seemed completely deserted. As soon as he had swept into the dance hall, the miners had scurried for cover, scrambling over each other in their efforts to hide from his deadly guns. Some of them were hiding behind the bar and others had taken refuge in barrels or behind tables and chairs.

Pierre laughed again. He had a loud laugh, one that filled the whole room, and seemed to bounce back and forth from the walls like huge claps of thunder. And it seemed to have the same threatening sound, only instead of carrying the threat of lightning it was backed up by a pair of smoking pistols that swept from one side of the room to the other.

But when the miners saw Pierre making advances to Minnie they raised up from their hiding places and began to fight. The air was soon sizzling with bullets and knives, and Pierre saw that he would have to make a break for cover. So, shooting out the lights, he fought his way to the door in darkness, with the girl under his arm and both

his guns spitting fire and lead.   Over the roar of the guns and the shouts of the enraged miners could be heard the booming sound of Pierre's laughter, and the gun flashes showed his face leering in the darkness like the evil monster he was.

As he reached the open air, Pierre gave a loud shout of triumph and slipped his guns into his belt.   Then, tying Minnie in his waiting dog sled, he cracked a long snakelike whip over the dogs' heads and cried "Moosh!"   The dogs jumped up, swayed from side to side to loosen the runners that had become frozen in the hard-packed snow, and away they went at top speed.   Up hill and down dale, threading his way along narrow trails and jumping yawning chasms, Pierre guided his dogs.   And at last they skidded to a stop in front of his cabin, high in the mountains.

Back in the dance hall, Mickey finally struggled loose from his position on the wall and rushed outside to where his faithful dog, Pluto, was hitched to a sled.   With a loud cry of "Mush!" they started after

Pierre.   Everything went smoothly until Pluto spied a rabbit bounding along the snow ahead of him.   He barked joyfully, laid back his ears, and started in pursuit, dragging the sled behind him.   Faster and faster went the rabbit, and faster and faster went the sled, with Mickey trailing out behind like the tail on a kite.   Then the rabbit darted into a hollow log and Pluto raced in after it.

WHAM!   The sled hit the log, went into a thousand pieces, and Mickey was sailing in the air before he knew what had happened.   But when he came down he landed on the runners of the sled, and, using them as skis, he continued the chase.   At last he reached the crest of a high hill, and far below him he saw Pierre's cabin, perched on the edge of a high bank.

Inside the cabin, Pierre was building a big fire when the door burst open and in flew Mickey on the skis.   He was going so fast that he sailed across the room, banged into a cupboard and crashed to the floor, almost buried under a shower of pots, pans and potatoes.   But

he jumped up, pointed at Pierre, and shouted: "Now I've got you, you cur!"

With a roar of anger Pierre rushed into the fight. And what a battle it was! All over the room they went, under the bed, up on the rafters and over chairs, with first one fighter gaining the upper hand and then the other.

But at last Pierre's strength began to tell on Mickey. His blows became weaker and weaker. It was getting harder to dodge the heavy blows aimed at him. He gasped for breath. But still he battled bravely. He made up his mind he would not quit as long as he could stand up on his two feet.

Meanwhile, Pluto was still chasing the rabbit. And what is more, he was gaining. But suddenly he slipped, tripped, and began rolling down the steep mountainside. Over and over he went, picking up loose snow as he rolled, until he was embedded in a giant snowball that grew bigger and bigger as it rushed down the mountain, straight for Pierre's cabin.

With a terrific crash the snowball hit the cabin, tearing it loose from its moorings and sending it slipping, sliding down the mountain, at breath-taking speed. And then—CRASH! The cabin hit a huge tree and broke into a million splinters. And that was the end of Pierre. When the wreckage came down, he was buried under a pile of logs and snow.

On top of the pile, into the soft snow, fell Mickey and Minnie and Pluto, unhurt and safe and very, very happy. It had been a grand fight and a grand adventure and another grand victory for Mickey Mouse, the Klondike Kid.

THE MAD DOCTOR

Mickey was restless. He tossed and turned in his bed, twisting from one side to the other. It was a poor night for sleeping. The wind whistled through the trees and moaned like a dog howling in the distance. Suddenly Mickey heard a howl that seemed louder than the wind. Then he heard it again, even louder. It sounded like Pluto! It WAS Pluto!

Mickey jumped out of bed and ran to the window. It was so black outside that he could not see what was happening, but he could hear Pluto's terrified cries fading in the distance.

Running like mad, Mickey fairly flew out to the back yard. A flash of lightning showed Pluto's overturned doghouse and a man's footprints disappearing toward the woods. With an agonized cry, Mickey started in pursuit.

Fighting his way against the wind, stumbling through the woods, tripping over gnarled roots, tearing himself loose from branches that tried to hold him back, Mickey followed the ruthless dognaper. And then, far in the distance, Mickey caught his first glimpse of his stolen dog. Pluto was being led across a narrow bridge into a huge evil-looking castle perched on a skull-like rock against which the angry sea was beating and pounding.

Mickey crossed the bridge in the nick of time, for just as he reached the castle door, the bridge gave way and crashed to the rocks far below.

Inside the castle Mickey looked around. It was a dark, spooky place. Cobwebs hung from the rafters, and the dying embers of a fire cast weird shadows on the rough stone wall. Bats flew around the ceiling, with a curious clicketty-clacking sound. Mickey looked up, startled, and what he saw made his hair stand on end. They weren't live bats at all! They were skeletons!

Mickey knew the house must be haunted, so he walked very slowly and gingerly down the long hall. Standing in a corner he saw an old grandfather's clock, whose pendulum was a skull that clicked its teeth together as it swung: Tick, tock, tick, tock. Out of the top of the clock popped a skeleton cuckoo. Mickey became more and more frightened until suddenly he heard Pluto howling. This drove all fear out of his mind. He could think of but one thing: he had to find his dog!

Climbing a low flight of stairs, Mickey started to peek through a round opening in the wall when WHOOOOSH! the stairs leveled off and Mickey slid to the floor. Not until then did he realize that a skeleton had been hiding under each step!

He rushed out of the room and down a long corridor, where he found a ladder leading up to the next floor. He fairly leapt at it and climbed as fast as he could make his hands and legs go. He was in such a hurry to find Pluto that he did not notice a skeleton perched on top of the

ladder. He climbed and climbed until suddenly he bumped his head on something. In an instant he saw what had happened and he gave a wild cry of fear! He had climbed up inside of the skeleton!

He started to run down a long hall, with the skeleton right with him. He dashed through a doorway and as he rounded a corner he slipped. When he fell down, the skeleton was broken into a dozen pieces. And away Mickey went, still trembling with fear, still looking for Pluto and still listening for a howl that would direct him to the dog. Then he heard it echoing down through the long hallways— such a terrified howl that it made his blood run cold.

No wonder Pluto was terrified. In another part of the castle he was strapped to the wall of a huge laboratory. Over his head was a poor little hen, chained to a coop. And facing him was The Mad Doctor!

The Doctor was a fiend in human form. It was he who had captured Pluto and dragged him to the castle. And as he looked at his victims

he laughed. It was a deep, hollow, mocking laugh—the laughter of an insane person. For the doctor was the maddest, craziest, most insane man that ever lived.

Throwing aside his black cloak, he took out a pair of scissors, a saw and a long knife which he began to sharpen. His eyes glittered as he began to speak:

"I'm very, very eager to start my cutting up,

And graft a chicken's gizzard to the wish-bone of a pup!"

At this, Pluto's mouth dropped open and his ears flew up straight. The doctor laughed again before he continued:

"And here's the great experiment I'm just about to tackle:

To find out if the net result will bark, or crow, or cackle!"

Then Pluto really DID howl! It was a long, wailing cry that filled the castle with sound from one end to the other.

This was the howl which Mickey had heard, and he stood puzzled, not knowing which way to turn. He was nearly frantic. He knew

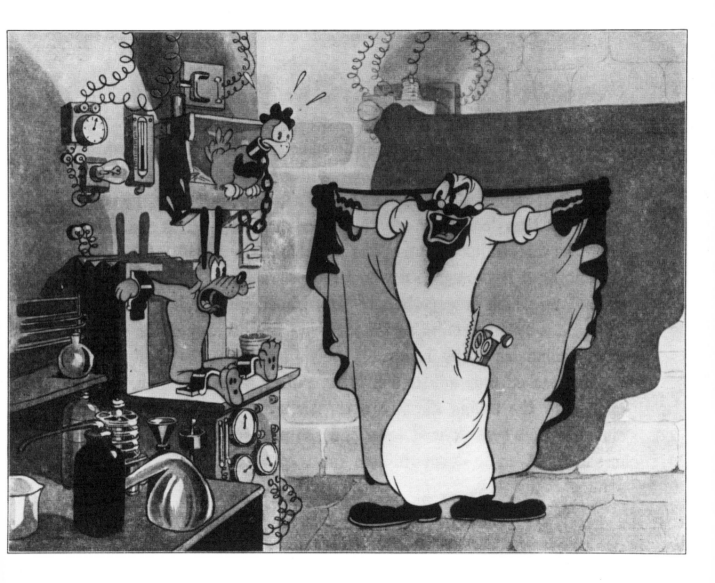

Pluto needed him and needed him badly. But how could he find the dog? Where was he? And what was happening to him?

These questions were answered sooner than Mickey expected. The stone floor on which he was standing suddenly opened up, and he dropped like a shot. Down a long slide he went, faster and faster, finally popping out a little trap door in the middle of the laboratory. The next thing he knew, he was strapped to an operating table under a brilliant flood-lamp.

The Mad Doctor gave a wild shriek of delight. Here was another patient on which to experiment. He rubbed his hands together gleefully. His eyes narrowed to the merest slits, and they glittered cruelly from behind his bushy brows.

He reached out, adjusted a lever, pulled down a switch. A door opened in the ceiling directly over Mickey's head. And as Mickey looked up his eyes popped open and the perspiration stood out on his forehead. Coming down through the trap door, straight at him, was a huge, whirling buzz-saw!

Closer, closer, closer it came. Mickey knew it was the end. He was strapped down. He could not move a muscle. He was absolutely helpless. Up above, he could hear the angry whir-r-r-r of the saw. In the distance, seemingly a mile away, he could hear Pluto howling dismally. And he could hear the Mad Doctor's crazy, high-pitched laughter.

Closer, closer, closer came the saw. Mickey began to pull in the muscles of his stomach—trying to make himself thinner—trying to ward off the approaching end. But he knew it was useless.

The tone of the saw was now a high, piercing whine. It was almost on him. He shut his eyes tightly. Five seconds to live! Four seconds! Three! Two! One! And then—

Mickey felt it touch his stomach! With an agonized cry of pain and terror, he opened his eyes! The laboratory was gone! The doctor's wild laughter was gone! Mickey blinked his eyes and looked around. He was in his own bedroom! Overhead, he saw a mosquito flying, and

he felt his tummy where the mosquito had just bitten him. So THAT was what the whirring sound had been! He sighed with relief, and grinned sheepishly. It had been a dream. But what a dream!

Outside, Pluto had heard Mickey's cry of fright. The faithful hound started for his master's room, dragging his doghouse behind him. Straight through the window he jumped, landing on the foot of Mickey's bed. Then, seeing that nothing was wrong, he plopped down beside Mickey and began to lick his face.

Pluto knew nothing about the dream. He only knew that his master had called him and that he had come as soon as he could.

And that, thought Mickey, was the best that ANY dog could do!

GULLIVER MICKEY

While his little nephews were playing around the living room in his house, Mickey Mouse sat in a big chair, reading "Gulliver's Travels." He loved to read books of adventure, for they stirred his imagination, and he always put himself in the hero's place. As he read, he could see himself doing all the things the story described—and more besides. Therefore, when the children tired of their play and asked him to tell them a story, Mickey laid his book aside and began to tell a fantastic tale that came partially from the book and partially from his own fertile imagination.

"It happened a long time ago," he said, "when I was just a little bit older than you are. One dark and stormy night I was ship-wrecked and cast up on the beach. I didn't know where I was, and I was so tired

from fighting the waves that I didn't care much. So I just stretched out and went sound asleep.

"Next morning, when I awoke, the storm had cleared up and the sun was shining, so I decided to explore a bit. But when I tried to sit up, I found I couldn't do it. I couldn't move a muscle. I was tied down, hand and foot, by dozens of strings that ran over my body and down to tiny stakes driven into the ground."

"Were ya scared?" asked one of his nephews.

"I was at first," Mickey answered, "but by turning my eyes a little I soon found out what had happened. I had been captured by an army of tiny little people just about as big as one of my fingers. And they had tied me down in a huge open court in the middle of their toy city.

"The streets were full of the little people, all of them jabbering at the tops of their funny, squeaky voices. They had never seen anybody like me, so they climbed up the ropes and crawled into my pockets, and walked back and forth all over me. It struck me funny and

I began to laugh. My tummy shook, like it always does when I laugh hard, and that broke all the strings that were holding me down. So I sat up and looked around me.

"All the little people ran away, 'cause they thought I might hurt them, or something. Then one very dignified, fat little fellow rode up on horseback and stopped beside me. I picked him up in my hand and held him out so that he could talk to me. He was awf'ly cute and so fat and funny and pompous that I couldn't help laughing. He unrolled a long scroll and began to read it, and his voice was very, VERY high and squeaky—a little tiny voice away up here—and of course that made me laugh harder than ever, 'cause he took himself so seriously.

"Naturally I couldn't understand a word he said, and he was so dignified and majestic that I thought I'd have some fun with him. So while he was giving his speech I rocked my hand, and bent my fingers and tickled him in the ribs. It made him furious, and when I

put him down on the ground he shouted something to the other people and they started into action.

"I guess he was a general, or something, and he must have given orders to the army, 'cause out of a little fort ran a whole lot of soldiers pulling the cutest little cannons you ever saw. They aimed 'em at me and started firing. Of course, they didn't hurt me much—I was so big, you see—but they did sting a little. So I got up and began to back away.

"It was a lot of fun, and they were all so very serious and brave that I wouldn't have hurt any of 'em for anything in the world. I had to be careful not to step on any of them as I headed for the ocean. But I finally made it, dodging the little bullets as I went.

"I waded out in the water up to my knees and then looked around. Coming toward me, around a nearby point, was the entire fleet—the cutest little boats you ever saw in your life. They were about as big as those ship models Uncle Mortimer used to make, and they were all quaint old fashioned boats—schooners with bright-colored sails, galleys

with long sweeping oars, and all of them manned by the tiny people. They meant business, too, for they came as fast as they could sail, all of them armed to the teeth and all of the guns aimed right at me.

"When they got within range, which was about ten feet, they started firing. The bullets stung me a little, like the ones in town did, but of course they didn't really hurt at all. So I went over and picked up one of the boats. Just as I did, the cannon in front went off and the bullet hit me right in the nose. That did hurt, for the cannon was only about a foot away. So when they loaded it again, I stuck my finger in the mouth of it, and when it went off it exploded.

"The poor sailors were almost scared to death, and they jumped overboard and started swimming for their lives. I didn't want to hurt 'em, of course, so I put the boat back in the water and scooped up all the sailors and very carefully placed them on the deck again. Then I blew on the sail and splashed water on the side of the boat so·it would have to go away and not bother me any more. I was having such a

good time with it that I didn't notice a galley speeding up behind me. I was stooped over looking at the sailboat when WHAM! the galley smacked me. I was so surprised that I let out a wild yell and jumped clear out of the water and up on land again.

"All the people began to cheer, for they thought they had me on the run. And they began to bring out more cannons and guns and giant bows and arrows and horses and all kinds of things. I couldn't dodge 'em all, of course, for there were too many of them. So I bent over and tried to cover my eyes, because that was the only place they could possibly have hurt me. And I was laughing so hard I couldn't have run anyway, so all I could do was just let 'em shoot to their hearts' content.

"While I had my eyes all covered up to protect them, the shooting suddenly stopped. And instead of the popping of guns, I heard a lot of terrified shouting. The people seemed scared of something. I thought they might be playing a trick on me, trying to get me to expose

myself or something, so I peeked out to see what was going on. And I saw that it was no trick. They were really scared. I couldn't understand it, for they had been so brave up to then. So I stood up to see what I had done to frighten them. And then I saw it! Coming along toward me, crawling over their houses and buildings, was the biggest spider that ever walked! He was almost half again as big as I was! And he was coming straight toward me, his face drawn in a ferocious growl of rage.

"No wonder the little people were scared. I was scared plenty myself. But the way to win a fight is to pitch right in and get it over with before the other fellow knows it's even started. So I jumped at the spider and let him have it with both fists. I socked him with my right, then my left, then my right and then my left. And then I uppercut him on the chin. He was wobbling and staggering, so I grabbed him by the legs and threw him clear out in the ocean. And that was the end of the spider."

"Is it the end of the story too?" asked one of his nephews.

"Yes, that's all there is," replied Mickey. "And what's more, anybody who doesn't believe it owes me a dime."

Without a word, all his nephews filed out of the room. At the door one of them turned and held out his hand. Mickey shook it gravely, and the little fellow left the house. Then Mickey stopped, puzzled, and looked at his outstretched hand.

In it was a shiny new dime!

BUILDING A BUILDING

Chiggetty-chuggetty! BANG! Toot-toot! Swish! CHUG! A giant steam-shovel swung around, opened its huge iron jaws, bit off a mouthful of dirt and rocks, and deposited the load in a waiting truck, filling it to the very brim. Another truck drove up and the operation was repeated. Down in the cabin Mickey Mouse was running the gigantic shovel. It was his job to dig the foundation for a new building, and he was having a grand time. It was lots of fun to be able to pick up so much dirt all at once, simply by pulling a series of little levers. It was like a game.

He was enjoying his work so much that he did not see a box lunch wagon drive up, nor did he see Minnie Mouse climb out of it. Minnie always arrived a little before lunchtime, selling her wares to the workmen on the building. As she walked up the scaffolding, she always sang a song:

"Box Lunch! Who'll buy a box lunch?
  They are good as good can be.
Box Lunch! Who'll buy a box lunch?
  Ev'ry one I'll guarantee.
Boloney, and macaroni—
  And pies that are sublime.
Try one; I know you'll buy one,
  Just a nickel and a dime!"

As she walked out on a girder, Minnie's hat blew off and fell down in the excavation where Mickey was working. Very deftly he picked up the bonnet with the steam shovel and gallantly handed it to her. She blushed and curtsied and he made the steam-shovel lift off its roof, as though it were tipping its hat.

Just then the noon whistle blew, and all work stopped.

As Mickey sat down to eat his lunch, Pete, the Foreman, peeked

down from his platform on the fourth floor. He saw Mickey's lunch box, far below, so he attached a hook to a long rope and lowered it. Mickey was watching Minnie and he did not see the hook fasten itself to his lunch box, nor did he see it disappear up to the waiting arms and hungry mouth of Pete. The first thing he knew about it was when he looked around. His lunch was gone!

Minnie saw the sorrowful look on his face. She picked out the best box lunch on her wagon and brought it over to him.

"Are you hungry?" she asked.

"Naw! Not very," he replied.

"Don't you want a box lunch?" she said, offering it to him.

"Yeah! But—but I haven't got any money," was the answer.

"I mean I wanted to GIVE it to you! Look!—Boloney, and macaroni, and huckleberry pie!" And she stuffed a big piece of pie into his mouth.

From his vantage point above, Pete was watching Mickey and Minnie. A wicked gleam came into his eye, and again he reached for

the rope to which the hook was attached. Lowering it carefully, he hooked it into Minnie's dress and suddenly hoisted her up to the platform on which he was standing.

"Hello, keed!" he said, laughing.

Minnie tried to slap him but when she swung her arm he ducked, and she spun around and around on the rope, which made Pete laugh harder than ever.

Anxious to protect his new-found friend, Mickey started up a ladder. Pete saw him coming. He picked up the ladder and spread it apart so that Mickey couldn't possibly climb it. Not discouraged, he jumped for a rope and went up it like lightning, hand over hand, arriving on the platform close behind Pete and Minnie. Pete was waiting for him. He grabbed Mickey, threw him down and began pounding his head on the wooden planks.

Minnie was terrified. She saw that Mickey was getting much the worst of the battle. She looked around and saw a small forge in which

rivets were heating. Grabbing a basket and a poker, she picked up a number of the rivets and ran back to where Pete was pummeling Mickey. With the poker Minnie pulled Pete's loose trousers back, and with her other hand she dropped the white-hot rivets inside.

"YOW-W-W-W-W-W!"

Pete jumped up with a terrific howl of pain, rushed over to a barrel of water and poured the contents down after the rivets. By the time he had cooled them off he was boiling with rage, and he had made up his mind to get Mickey and Minnie if it was the last thing he ever did.

They, of course, had started to get away. They ran along the platform and climbed up a ladder leading to the framework of the floor above. On reaching it, Mickey threw the ladder down to the ground so that Pete could not follow them. However, Pete ran along under them, shaking his fist and cursing at the top of his voice. He spied a big riveting gun, and using it as a machine gun he started firing hot rivets at them.

RAT-A-TAT-A-TAT-A-TAT! CLANGETTY-CLANGETTY-CLANG! The rivets tore through a steel girder as if it were made of cardboard. Mickey and Minnie were on the girder, and as they ran it was shot off behind them. Pete laughed loudly and started to raise the gun so that the rivets would hit Mickey and Minnie instead of the girder. There is no telling what might have happened, for just as he raised his sights he tripped. Down he went, flat on his back. The gun flew up in the air and came down on his wooden leg, attaching itself with the business end down!

The gun was still going full blast; when Pete started to run he jiggled and bounced around as though he were standing on an electric vibrator.

There was no chance to catch Mickey and Minnie now, for with the riveting gun on his leg Pete jiggled up and down just as much as he went ahead. And if he stopped to take it off, it would give them such a head-start that he never would be able to overtake them. So he stopped. And that was his undoing. The riveter cut through the

girder on which he was standing, and he fell through the hole it made. On his way to the ground he smashed into a small concrete mixer and took it along with him.

Down, down, down he went, crashing into girders and planks, head over heels and heels over head, finally landing on the ground, far below, in a pile of wreckage. He was all through for the day. He didn't care WHAT happened to Mickey and Minnie now. All he wanted was some arnica to rub on his bruises.

At first, when they saw him falling, Mickey and Minnie were worried. But when they saw him land, not much the worse for wear, they laughed delightedly. They were safe at last.

They jumped into a little cart and headed for a concrete-chute that led to the ground. WHIZ-Z-Z-Z! ZIP-P-P-P! Just like a chute-the-chutes, they zoomed downward, whirling around corners and swishing along the straightaways until they came to a stop in a long trough where plaster was being mixed.

Mickey jumped out and helped Minnie as she stepped daintily from the "boat." He escorted her to her little box lunch cart. When she got in she asked him to join her. Mickey didn't wait for a second invitation, but jumped over the rear end.

As they rode down the street, Minnie stuck her finger in a juicy huckleberry pie. With the red juice she added Mickey's name to the sign on back of her cart. It now read: "MICKEY'S AND MINNIE'S BOX LUNCHES."

She smiled. Then she blushed and held up her lips so that Mickey could seal the new partnership with a kiss.

And, so far as I know, they are still partners!

MICKEY'S PAL, PLUTO

Pluto was the happiest dog in the world. He was out walking with Mickey and he bounded along through the snow on the river bank, barking joyfully.

Suddenly he stopped. Out in the river was a cake of ice on which was resting a large burlap sack. As he watched he saw it moving. There was something alive in it. He plunged into the water and swam out to the ice. Soon he was on his way back to shore, dragging the bag behind him.

"What ya got, Pluto?" asked Mickey, helping the dog out of the water. And then, "Well, I'll be—! It's full o' kittens! Aw, th' poor things! They're nearly frozen. C'mon, ol' feller, let's take 'em home an' see if we can warm 'em up."

So saying, Mickey picked them all up and hurried home, with Pluto trotting along proudly, very pleased with himself.

Mickey and Minnie dried the kittens and soon the little fellows were playing and scampering all over the room. Pluto thought it was great fun, and started to play with them. However, one kitten reached out a paw and scratched him on the nose. Pluto stopped, then straightened up, astonished. Mickey turned around just in time to see the strange look on Pluto's face, and Mickey thought he was angry rather than surprised.

"Now, Pluto," he cautioned, shaking his finger at the dog. "Don't you hurt those kittens."

Pluto's jaw dropped in amazement. He hadn't meant to hurt the kittens. He only wanted to play with them. A little lump came to his throat, so he went over to his bowl to get a drink. It was full of kittens, not only drinking the milk but wading around in it. Feeling his temper rising, Pluto decided he would be wise to get clear out of the way, so he started toward his bed in the corner. But it, too, was full of kittens.

Suddenly there was a tiny puff of smoke close beside Pluto, and up through the floor popped a little Demon. It was Pluto's Bad Self! The Demon pointed at the kittens and said:

"Chase those cats away from here,
  Or you'll get thrown out on your ear!"

Pluto started to snarl, and he was about to follow the Demon's advice when down from the ceiling floated an Angel. It was Pluto's Good Self—his Conscience. It said:

"Don't take that Demon's bad advice!
  Be a good dog. Treat them nice."

Pluto was torn between two fires. He wanted to chase the kittens, yet he knew he shouldn't. The Angel continued:

"Have patience, Pluto! Don't be cross!"

"Aw, that guy's full of apple-sauce!" replied the Demon.

"They'll steal your home! So do your stuff!

Chase 'em out, and treat 'em rough!"

Pluto was worried. He knew that if he allowed the kittens to stay in the house they might steal his home, his dinner—even his bed. Yet if he started to chase them, Mickey would be very angry, and Pluto would probably lose his home anyway. So he did the wise thing. He simply went outdoors.

He had been outside but a few minutes when he looked up, amazed. The kittens were sneaking out of a little hole under a corner of the house. They headed across the yard, with Pluto following them. He saw them climb up on the side of a deep well. They jumped into the bucket playfully. And then—He saw the bucket sink slowly down into the well!

He jumped up on the side of the well and looked down. There, swimming helplessly around in the icy water, were the kittens. Pluto didn't know what to do. Should he try to rescue them himself or should he go and get Mickey? Or should he——?

But before he had a chance to answer his own question, he saw the Angel drift down beside him, and heard it say:

"Save them, Pluto! Save those cats!

Don't let the poor things drown like rats!"

Pluto started to reach for the rope, and pull the kittens up to safety, but as he did so, there was a puff of smoke, and the Demon appeared, shouting:

"Leave them there! Don't be a clown!

They're only kittens; let 'em drown!"

Again Pluto's mind was in a whirl. He knew he couldn't be blamed if the kittens drowned. He had nothing to do with their being in the well. And with them out of the way, the house would be his again. Maybe that WOULD be best. And yet—

"You MUST save them!" cried the Angel, his Conscience.

"Don't you do it!" commanded the Demon, his Bad Self.

"Yes!" shouted the Angel. "No!" replied the Demon. "Yes!" "No!" "Yes!" "No!" "Yes!" "No!" "Yes!"

"Aw, you make me sick," said the Demon. And before the Angel

could defend himself, the Demon hit him a terrific blow in the face, almost knocking him down in the well.

"See?" snarled the Demon. "He can dish it out, but he can't take it!"

Pluto began to scowl. His Bad Self was overcoming his Conscience. It must be true. His Conscience was just a sissy.

But the Angel thought differently. "Can't take it, huh?" he shouted. "Well, how do you like THIS?"

So saying, he rushed at the Demon, with both fists swinging.

"Or this?" He planted his fist deep in the Demon's stomach. "Or this?" He swung a hard left to the point of the jaw. "Or this?" And he lifted his fist in a terrific uppercut that sent the Demon spinning head over heels through the air, where he landed in a heap in a nearby garbage can.

Pluto's Conscience had won over his Bad Self.

"Now, Pluto," cried the Angel, "grab that rope and save them!"

Pluto did. He took the rope between his teeth and pulled the kittens up to safety. But in doing so he slipped, lost his balance and fell into the well himself. And there he was, hanging onto the rope for dear life, hoping and praying that Mickey would arrive before his strength gave way.

Mickey and Minnie heard the rumpus outside, and they rushed over to the well. Minnie gathered the kittens in her skirt and together she and Mickey started back toward the house, not knowing that Pluto was down in the well!

Poor Pluto! He knew he had to bark to save himself. But if he opened his mouth he would fall down into the icy water. However, he had to take a chance.

"OWP! OWP! OWOOOOOOOOOOO-blubble-blubble-blubble!"

Mickey stopped short. "Pluto!" he cried. "He's in the well!"

Rushing over, he grabbed the rope and pulled his faithful dog up to safety.

"Pluto!" he said. "You're—you're a HERO!"

Pluto shivered and licked his master's face happily.

"Kittens are all right for GIRLS," Mickey went on, "but for ME, I want a real, good, faithful dog who's brave enough an' who's got sense enough to do what you just did!"

Then he picked Pluto up in his arms and tenderly carried him into the house, where he brought a whole turkey for the dog to eat. Pluto was perfectly happy. He sniffed at the turkey. Then he looked at it again, and his eyes popped open in astonishment. There, standing on it, was the Angel, saying:

"Kindness always pays, my friend,
  You'll be rewarded in the end."

Folding its hands benevolently, the Angel disappeared, leaving Pluto alone. And the dog smiled again as he took a huge mouthful of the turkey. He knew the Angel was right.

TOUCHDOWN MICKEY

"SIGNALS!"

Mickey crouched down behind the center.

"82–44–37–91—SHIFT!" he called. With the precision of a machine, his linesmen moved into new positions.

"Two—four—six—eight—ELEVEN—HIKE!" Back came the ball to Mickey's arms. He dove into a hole between guard and tackle. But the hole closed up suddenly, and down he went under a pile of arms and legs and bodies.

Crawling out and shaking his head to clear it, Mickey glanced up at the scoreboard. It read: Mickey's Manglers 82, Alley Cats 94. Two touchdowns behind, and only three minutes to play!

Again Mickey called for the ball, and away he went around the end—five, ten, fifteen yards. The crowd nearly went wild, thinking

he was getting away for another touchdown. But one of the Alley Cats grabbed him by the ankle, and he was instantly buried under an avalanche of players.

Time was getting short, so Mickey decided to gamble. Taking the ball from center he pretended to be running with it. Just as he was about to be tackled he flipped a quick forward pass into the arms of an end. A dozen strides and the end was over the goal line for a touchdown. Mickey kicked goal and the score was now 89 to 94—still one touchdown behind and less than two minutes to play.

Calling time out, Mickey's team trotted over to the sidelines for a much-needed rest. Grabbing sponges and dippers, they soused themselves, and soon were lined up again out on the field.

While they were refreshing themselves the Alley Cats went into a huddle and planned some foul strategy. They plastered a coating of slippery mustard on the ball, knowing this would make it almost impossible to catch. Then they elected to kick off.

The referee's whistle blew, and PLOOMP! the ball sailed through the air toward the waiting arms of Halfback Spitz, who got set to catch it. WHOOSH! down it came, and z-z-zip! it slipped through his fingers, bounding crazily around near the goal line. Mickey dove on it, but the mustard-covered ball slithered through his hands. He was after it in a flash, but so was the entire Alley Cat team. Mickey got there first, with the Alley Cats right behind him. And no sooner had he hit the ground than they piled up on him, tugged at the ball and nearly pulled his clothes off of him. There was such a hogpile that the referee could not see what was going on under it. And when he finally pulled off the Alley Cats, one of them had the ball and poor Mickey was almost knocked out.

Alley Cats' ball on Mickey's five yard line. First down, four yards to go and one minute to play. Seventeen—seventy-six—eighteen—twelve—WHAM! No gain!

Again they lined up, again the Alley Cat quarterback shouted his

signals and again Mickey's Manglers stopped them with no gain. But the timekeeper's watch ticked on relentlessly. Ten seconds to go; time for only one more play!

The Alley Cats smiled happily. They were sure they had won the game. But with Mickey, the game was never over until the final gun had sounded. Until then he always played his hardest, no matter what the score was. He knew his only chance now was to hit the ball-carrier so hard he would fumble. He gritted his teeth in determination as he crouched behind the line.

The ball was snapped. The fullback started around the end. Mickey darted in like a streak of lightning and CRASH! the two players came together. The fullback went over backwards and the ball squirted out of his hands. Mickey jumped to his feet and was after it like a flash. He scooped it up on the dead run and started for the distant goal.

The entire Alley Cat team was upon him, however, and he had to fight and twist and squirm and tug to get away from them. One had

him by the knees, another had him by the belt, another was diving on him from above and two or three more were coming from every side. It looked like an impossible task. But Mickey had done even more impossible things than this. He spun around like a top, jumped sideways, stiff-armed a would-be tackler and before the Alley Cats knew what had happened he was out in the clear, with only two men between him and the goal. Only two men standing between defeat and victory!

The crowd was going wild. Women screamed, men cheered and threw their hats in the air, and there was a mixture of every animal sound that could be imagined. The radio announcer nearly went crazy. All he could say was:

"Mickey's away! He's away! He's down! He's up! He's down! He's up again! Oh, boy! what a game! What a game!"

Running like a madman, Mickey headed down the field, with the ball tucked under his arm. Five, ten, fifteen, twenty yards he raced at

top speed. An opposing halfback gained on him, almost reached him, but just as he dove Mickey sidestepped and the halfback crashed to the ground.

The other halfback was coming up fast. He was one of the two men between Mickey and the goal. With his huge arms outstretched, he lunged at Mickey. But Mickey jumped sideways, spun around in the air. He almost got away, but as he came down he tripped and went rolling, end over end. He tried to get up in time to dodge the remaining player. But it was too late. The Alley Cat quarterback grabbed him by the trousers as he went by.

Putting his head down, Mickey strained and tugged his way toward the goal. And CRASH! down he went, right in front of the goal line, with his face buried in the dirt. But the ball, held in his outstretched arms, was safely over the goal line!

BANG! went the timer's gun—and the game was over. The score-board read: Mickey's Manglers 95, Alley Cats 94.

Then the crowd really DID go mad. It surged out on the field, and Mickey was immediately surrounded by a crazy, cheering mob. He was lifted high in the air, perched on the goalposts, and paraded from one end of the field to the other.

A little figure slipped through the crowd and climbed up on the posts beside him. It was Minnie!

"Hurray! Hurray! He's all right! Who's all right? MICKEY!" shouted the crowd.

But Mickey didn't hear a word of it. All he could hear was a tiny voice whispering in his ear. And all he could see was the cutest girl in the world sitting close beside him, holding his hand tightly in hers.

No wonder he smiled so happily. Who wouldn't have?

MICKEY'S MECHANICAL MAN

This was the big night! Mickey's Mechanical Man was to fight the Champion of the World, the Kongo Killer, in the Battle of the Century. The Kongo Killer was a big gorilla, so ferocious and so strong that no human could possibly defeat him. Mickey had built a mechanical man, and had trained him and oiled him and greased him until he was in perfect shape for the fight.

Minnie Mouse drove up alongside the training quarters in her little auto. Seeing the "No Admittance" signs all over the building, she blew her horn for Mickey:

TA-TAAAA-TUH-TAAAAAAAA!

Wham! Out through the side of the building burst the robot. He was crazy with rage. He had turned into a wild, mechanical demon, and he was pulling up telephone poles and swinging his fists at everything in sight.

Mickey rushed out after him and saw Minnie laughing merrily.

"Aw, gee, Minnie," he cried. "Please don't blow that horn any more. It drives him CRAZY!"

Of course Minnie promised she wouldn't, so together they chased the robot down the street, finally picking him up beside a brick wall on which was a picture of the Kongo Killer. The mechanical man had attacked the poster, but the brick wall had been too much for even his mighty efforts to overcome.

He was pretty badly battered, and some of his muscles were bent and dented. So Mickey rushed him down to the arena, where he made some last-minute repairs. He had just finished shooting the final drop of oil into the robot's right knee when it was time for the big fight to get under way.

Once in the ring, the mechanical man seemed to be himself again. He danced and pranced very gracefully, shooting out his gloves like a masterful boxer. The only trouble was, they didn't come anywhere

near the Kongo Killer. The gorilla didn't know what to make of it at first. He sidled around, waiting to see what would happen. He didn't have long to wait. The mechanical man's telescopic right arm shot out about ten feet, and socked the gorilla a terrific blow on the chin.

With a wild bellow of rage, the Kongo Killer went into action. Rights and lefts and uppercuts rained all over the steel man's body and head. The poor robot didn't have a chance against such a demoniacal fury. An uppercut to the chin stretched his neck out about three feet and a terrific blow on top of the head folded him up again like an accordion. The Kongo Killer picked him up by the legs and slammed him down to the floor, scattering springs and cog wheels all over the canvas. He managed to get up again, but he was staggering and weaving. As he struggled to his feet he met another shower of blows. His head spun around on his neck, his right arm dangled uselessly at his side, and a bolt was loose in his left knee, causing him to limp badly.

Again the Kongo Killer rushed in. Again he lifted the robot above his head. He whirled him around and around, and this time when the mechanical man crashed to the floor he was unable to get up. As a matter of fact, he did not even try to get up. His eyes were bleary. His parts were scattered all around him. He was almost in pieces—like an auto after a bad wreck. As he lay on the floor, little mechanical birdies flew around over his head. He was absolutely knocked out.

The referee's voice began droning the count. One . . . two . . . Mickey begged his fighter to get up. "Come on!" he shouted. "We'll win this fight YET!" But his voice was lost in the howls of the audience. Three . . . Four . . .

Mickey looked around and saw that Minnie had left. Where had she gone? Five . . . Six . . . Mickey saw her running down the aisle. In her hand she was carrying the horn from her auto. He saw at once what she was planning to do. At last! A ray of hope!

Seven . . . Eight . . . Minnie poked the horn in the robot's ear and pressed the bulb.

TA-TAAAA-TUH-TAAAAAAAA!

The mechanical man's eyes popped open. His fists clenched. NINE. . . . He jumped to his feet. And then, for the first time, he really started to fight.

He fought with his fists and he fought with his feet. His mouth flew open, and out shot a spare boxing glove that hit the gorilla in the face. A trap door in his stomach opened up, and out popped three gloves that hit the Kongo Killer in quick succession.

The champion began to back away. He had never had anything like this happen before, and he didn't know how to fight back. Every time he would start to hit the robot, he would be socked in the face by a dozen boxing gloves that seemed to come from everywhere at once.

Biff! Bang! Wham! Splat! Sock! The Kongo Killer tried to get away, but he was no match for the enraged robot, who was working

like an angry piece of machinery—which, of course, is exactly what he was.

The crowd was in a frenzy of excitement. They threw their hats in the air, jumped up and down on their chairs and shrieked at the top of their lungs.

"Atta boy!" Mickey yelled. "Give it to 'im! Whoopee!"

The mechanical man WAS giving it to him! The Kongo Killer was trying his best to get somewhere else just as fast as he could. He attempted to jump the ropes, but the robot reached out one of his long arms and dragged him back. With the other arm he unloosed a series of punches that rattled against the gorilla's body with the speed of a machine gun. The Kongo Killer had started the unfair fighting, and he was now getting more of it than he wanted. He was getting a nice big dose of his own medicine, and it tasted horribly bitter.

Remembering how the gorilla had picked him up by the feet and smashed him down on the canvas, the mechanical man decided to try

the trick himself.   In he rushed, and grabbed the Kongo Killer by his feet.   Then around and around and around his head he swung him, while the gorilla howled in terror.   At last, with a mighty heave, the mechanical man let go his grip, and the gorilla went up, up, up—through the ceiling and through the roof.   Back he came, landing on a rafter, where he lay in safety, if not in comfort.   He refused to come back down, so the referee counted him out where he lay.

The mechanical man was so furious that he went completely crazy. He tore all around the ring, swinging his fists, and kicking and jumping and socking so hard that he couldn't dodge his own blows!   One of them landed on his chin so viciously that he knocked himself out and showered his parts all over the ring.   There he lay: nuts, bolts, screws, springs and baling wire, scattered from one side of the canvas to the other.

The referee didn't quite know what to do.   Obviously, the mechanical man had won, and his hand should be raised in victory.   But it was hard to locate the hand in the pile of junk the robot had made of

himself. He called Mickey up to help locate the missing part, and when they found it he raised Mickey's hand as well as the robot's, and shouted to the crowd:

"Introducing, folks, the new world's champion: Mickey's Mechanical Man!"

When the cheering and laughter had subsided, he went on:

"It just shows what may happen if you lose your temper! You're liable to go all to pieces—just like this fellow did!"

SHANGHAIED

As Captain Pegleg Pete's ship sailed out of the harbor in the early dawn, Pete went to his cabin to see the two unwilling passengers bound and gagged there. The night before, his sailors had shanghaied them and taken them aboard, to become cabin boy and maid during the voyage.

Pete laughed as he saw Mickey and Minnie struggling to get loose. He eyed Minnie evilly, appraising her from head to foot, then advanced and untied the bandage on her mouth.

"Mmmmmm! Nice!" he said, chucking her under the chin.

As Mickey tried to slip from his bonds, his chair tipped over and broke a bottle on the floor. Lying on his side, Mickey scraped a rope against a piece of the broken glass. One strand separated. Another one! The rope parted! He was free!

Rushing across the room, he grabbed a knife on the table and jabbed Pete in the rear. Pete let out a wild roar, jumped up to the ceiling, and came down with his peg leg stuck in the bottom part of Mickey's chair. Before he had time to collect his wits, Mickey cut Minnie's ropes and shooed her out of the cabin.

Pete grabbed a huge sword and started for Mickey, bellowing with rage. He had a hard time managing his right leg, however, for every time he put it down the casters on Mickey's chair rolled along like a skate. Mickey dodged all his blows, for he could turn much faster than Pete. But he realized that one of Pete's wild swings might connect, and if it did . . . no more Mickey!

He stood up on a little rocking chair and made a derisive face at Pete, who was so angry that he rushed at Mickey full speed ahead. Just as he was about to be run through by the sword, Mickey tipped the chair over backwards, and Pete was caught between the rockers, sailing over and landing flush on his face.

While Pete was untangling himself, Mickey ran out of the cabin, found Minnie, attached a rope to her, and hoisted her up the main-mast, where she hid on a yardarm, high above the deck. Then he hid himself in a barrel, waiting to see what would happen.

He did not have to wait long. Pete stormed out of the cabin, put his fingers to his lips and whistled shrilly. Then he bellowed at the top of his voice: "On deck, yuh swabs!"

Immediately the deck was swarming with cutthroat sailors, armed to the teeth, ready to obey the captain's commands.

"Git them little rats!" Pete shouted. "Bring 'em to me, dead or alive!" He paused and looked around at the sailors. "Well—what are yuh waitin' for? Git goin'!"

The sailors wasted no time. They began to search the ship from bow to stern. Mickey knew he would be discovered. He knew that if captured he would be made to walk the plank. Therefore he made up his mind that he would not be taken alive.

"If I've got to die," he said, climbing out of the barrel, "I'm sure going to take some of those guys with me!"

As he made his way across the deck and scampered up to the roof of a cabin, he was seen by a group of sailors huddled below. They started after him with a triumphant roar.

Mickey looked around for some kind of weapon with which to defend himself. The only article near him was an old battered stove that had been discarded. But a good fighter makes use of whatever weapons are at hand. And Mickey was a good fighter. He shoved the stove against a rope ladder, then got behind and pulled it back as far as he could. As the sailors swarmed across the deck, he let fly. The ladder acted as a catapult, and the stove sailed through the air, making a perfect bull's-eye in the midst of the howling crew.

Minnie heard the crash and the cries, and peeked over the yardarm to see what had happened. Her slight movement caught the eye of Pegleg Pete, who had also heard the noise and who had come to investigate it.

Shouting with glee, he pedaled his way across the deck like a small boy on a scooter. Reaching the mast, he attached a hook to the seat of his trousers and started pulling himself up the mast, using the casters for wheels.

He was roaring with laughter. He had Minnie right where he wanted her. She was perched on the yardarm. That was as far as she could go. She was helpless. There she was, and there she had to stay. And as for Mickey, Pete knew the crew would take care of HIM! So up he went, now chuckling to himself, now bellowing with anticipated pleasure.

Poor Minnie! She knew she didn't have a chance. She crept along the yardarm to the extreme end. She was so frightened she could not make a sound. And Pete was coming closer . . . closer . . . closer! As he reached the yardarm, she jumped up and caught hold of a rope that swung above her head. As Pete reached out for her she shrieked at the top of her voice.

Down below, Mickey heard her cry for help. He looked up and took

in the whole situation at a glance. He knew he could not go up the mast and rescue Minnie. True, he might be able to overcome Pete, but if he did the crew would gather around the mast and he and Minnie would never be able to get down alive. He would have to get rid of Pete by some other method.

He glanced around. In a box near him he saw a number of signal rockets, for use when a ship is in distress.

"Well, if ever a ship was in distress, THIS one is," he thought. "And maybe—!" He looked up again. Pete was straddling the mast like a child riding pick-a-back. Mickey smiled grimly and placed the rocket at the base of the mast, directly under the captain's bulging trousers. Then, touching a lighted match to the fuse, he stood back to watch results.

Pete had just grabbed Minnie's foot and was trying to pull her to him when Mickey lit the skyrocket. The fuse sputtered for a few seconds, and then—

F-f-f-f-ft! Spiz-z-z-z-zt! Wh-h-h-h-ISH-H-H-H-H-H-H-H!!!

The rocket leaped into the air like a thing alive. Pete was taken utterly by surprise. More than that, he was taken by the rocket— taken straight up the mast, through the crow's nest, and high into the air. Then the rocket burst, as rockets do, with a long AH-H-H-H-H-h-h -h-h-h sound, and Pete became the central figure in a beautiful display of many-colored stars. He started falling about the time the stars burned out, and from then on he was all by himself. But he was far from beautiful.

He lit on top of the after-deck housing, badly battered, much the worse for wear, and with very little fight left in him. The crew, how-ever, was full of fight. The men crept along the deck on their hands and knees, in single file, intent only on capturing Mickey. But Mickey, acting with the speed of lightning, had located a small cannon. In it he had loaded a harpoon, to which was attached a long rope. He aimed the harpoon just above the advancing sailors and pulled the trigger.

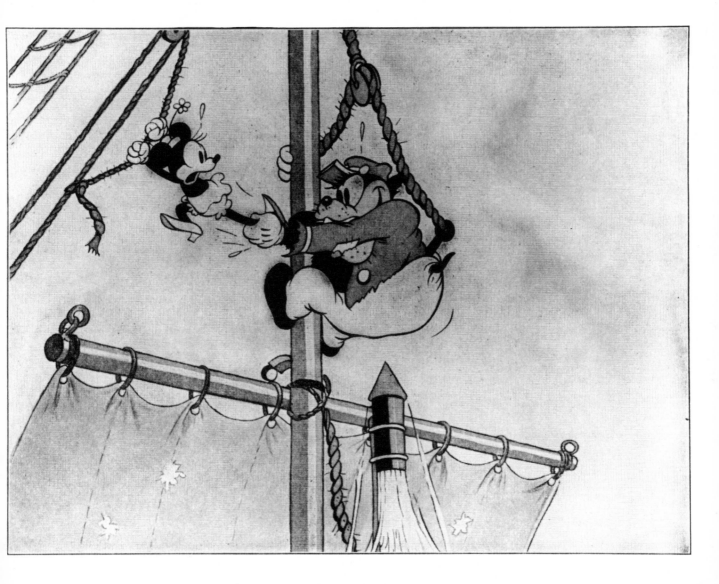

ZIP-P-P-P-P! The harpoon sailed through the air, threaded its way through each sailor's trousers, and smacked squarely into Pete, who was still perched on the after-deck housing.

So strong was the force of the harpoon that it carried Pete and the housing far out in the ocean, leaving the sailors dangling like so many wet clothes on a clothesline.

The battle was over. Mickey had won single-handed. So, with Minnie by his side again, he turned the ship around and headed for home, towing the sailors behind. When they arrived, the entire crew was thrown in jail.

And, so far as I know, they are still there.

MICKEY'S STEAMROLLER

The main street of town was being re-paved. Gangs of workmen drilled into the old pavement, cutting it up into long, irregular slabs. Giant steam shovels picked up the slabs and tossed them into waiting trucks. Other trucks dumped huge loads of sand, gravel and cement, which were piled every few yards down the length of the street. Ditch-diggers dug long, deep trenches into which gas and sewer pipes were to be laid. And, coming down the middle of the street, was a big steamroller, with Mickey Mouse at the helm.

CHUGGETTY-PUFF-ka-CHUG-ka-puff! TOOT! TOOT! CHUG! Ka-PUFF!

It was Mickey's job to smooth down the dirt after the pavement had been removed, to make it ready for the new concrete. As he drove along, he waved a cheery greeting to the workmen.

Mickey enjoyed driving the steamroller. It gave him a feeling of power. He liked to take it over rough ground and then turn around and see the smooth, floor-like path it left behind him. Of course it wouldn't go as fast as he usually liked to travel, but it had lots of other things to make up for it.

TOOT! TOOT! CHUGGETTY-PUFF! CHUG! PUFF! CLING! CLANG! CHIGGETTY-CHUGGETTY! PUFF! CHUG! TOOT! TOOT! CHUG! CHUG!

Backward and forward, over and over again, Mickey rolled the street until it was as smooth and hard and level as a table. Then he waved his hand at the inspector, as a signal that his work was finished and ready to be checked. The inspector looked up and down the street with a practised eye and nodded his head approvingly. Mickey was a good workman. He had done his job well. The inspector signaled the concrete men to start their part of the work. So with a terrific

grinding and clanging and swishing, the giant concrete mixer began to turn out volumes of soft new concrete.

Mickey's work was finished for the time being, so he started up the street. He had gone only a few blocks when his eyes popped open and a delighted smile lit up his entire face. What he saw was Minnie Mouse, dressed in a nurse's outfit, taking two small children out for a ride in the park.

Minnie saw him about the same time he saw her. She stopped and waved her hand at him.

"Yoo-hoo!" she called. And for answer, Mickey blew a loud blast on his whistle.

As the steamroller snorted up and hissed to a stop alongside of them, the children were so excited they jumped up and down in their baby carriage.

"Take us for a ride, Unca Mickey!" they shouted. "We want a ride! Ride! Ride!"

Mickey looked at Minnie. "Would it be all right?" he asked. When

she nodded, he jumped out and attached a heavy rope to the front of the baby carriage.

"You ride inside with me," he explained to Minnie, "an' we'll tow the kids along behind."

No sooner said than done. Minnie climbed up in the cab, Mickey rang the bell, and away they went with the children shrieking for joy. They were having the ride of their lives. But after awhile one of them spied a drinking fountain down the street.

"Hey! Unca Mickey!" he shouted. "We want a drink!"

Mickey obligingly pulled over to the curb by the fountain and they all climbed out. The children took the first drinks, and while Minnie and Mickey were leaning over the fountain, the children decided to investigate the steamroller. They clambered up over the rear end and were soon inside the cabin.

They looked around admiringly. It was the first time either had ever been so close to a steamroller, and it was most interesting. They

looked in the firebox, which was shooting out hot flames. They looked at the wheels and levers and gauges and pretended they knew all about them. One of the boys spied a pair of Mickey's gloves and his cap. He put them on and proudly showed them to his brother.

"Now I'm Unca Mickey!" he said. "Watch me drive the steamroller!"

So saying, he reached up and pulled back the lever.

With a slow CHOCK-CHOCK-CHOCK the steamroller started lumbering down the street.

Mickey and Minnie saw it moving, and both realized what had happened. Minnie screamed, and Mickey dashed over to stop it. But he didn't have a chance.

"Whee!" cried the boy at the lever. "Look! We're GOING!" He reached up and blew a long blast on the whistle.

"Now let's go FAST!" he said. And he pulled the lever back as far as it would go.

With a terrific roar, the steamroller answered the lever. Huge clouds of black smoke belched from the smokestack, and small puffs of steam hissed from its bulging sides. Faster, faster, faster went the roller, with Mickey running behind, doing his best to catch up. He did manage to catch hold of the baby carriage, but the second boy unhooked it and left Mickey helpless.

CHIGGETTY - CHUGGETTY - CHIGGETTY - CHUGGETTY - CHIGGETTY-CHUGGETTY!

"Do ya wanna go backwards?" shouted the boy. And he pushed the lever the other direction, as far as it would go.

CHIGGETTY - CHUGGETTY - CHIG - CHUG - CHUG - CHO - O-O-OSHHHH! It came to a stop. Then, slowly at first, but rapidly gaining speed, it began to back up. CHUG - CHUG - CHIG - A - CHUG - A - CHIG - A - CHIG - A - CHIGGETTY - CHUGGETTY - CHIGGETTY - CHUGGETTY - CHIGGETTY - CHUGGETTY . . .

Mickey had almost caught up to the roller again. Then he saw it

backing up, right at him. He skidded to a stop, and barely managed to jump aside as the roller whizzed by.

The boys were having a grand time. They blew the whistle and rang the bell and shouted and squealed with delight. The steamroller wasn't used to such treatment. It began to get angry. It headed for trees, which it crushed and flattened like so many pancakes. It fairly leaped up the curbing and smashed the drinking fountain to bits. Every time it broke something the boys blew the whistle and shrieked with laughter. Backwards and forwards they took the roller until Mickey was nearly frantic.

Finally the boys discovered how to steer it. That made it even more fun. And what a good time they could have chasing Unca Mickey! So they did it!

Poor Mickey. Now he had to run for his very life. Up the street, around corners, and over the crest of a hill he ran. Down the hill, with the steamroller gaining at every stride. He looked over his shoulder.

It was almost upon him. His only chance was to get inside an old deserted hotel at the bottom. So in he dashed.

The roller tried to follow. WHAM! C-R-R-RASH! With a roar, the hotel went to pieces and fell around the steamroller.

Thinking the children had been killed, Mickey was panic-stricken. Minnie arrived, pushing the baby carriage, in time to help him search the ruins for them. She was crying. Mickey was burrowing into the wreckage like a mole.

Then Minnie looked up. She rubbed her eyes. Both children were sitting in the baby carriage, innocently sucking their thumbs. They had sneaked out of the débris and had climbed into the carriage, unseen by Mickey and Minnie.

Because he was so full of mischief himself, Mickey couldn't get very angry at them. And all Minnie did was give them a good lecture. So off they went, with not even a bruise to show for their exciting adventure and their narrow escape.

But as for the steamroller, it never looked the same again.

YE OLDEN DAYS

In days of old, when knights were bold,
    And ladies all were gay,
A jolly minstrel strummed his uke,
    And sang this merry lay:

"I am a wand'ring minstrel,
    I journey from afar.
My worldly goods are a sleepy old mule,
    A song and a busted guitar!"

Without a care in the world, Minstrel Mickey rode his little donkey across the drawbridge that led to the inner courtyard of the king's castle.   Hearing sounds of merriment inside, he vaulted from his mule up onto the back of a horse, and peeked in the high window.

Inside, he saw the king sitting on his gilded throne, addressing the court:

"Oh, hear ye, loyal subjects
Of my kingdom of Lalapazoo!
Upon this day my daughter weds
The Prince of Poopoopadoo!"

There came a blast of trumpets and a page's voice: "Behold! The Prince!" From the opposite end of the courtroom came a similar blast and another voice: "Behold! The Princess!"

Long velvet curtains were parted and the prince and princess entered the room, advancing until they met directly in front of the throne. The princess was the cutest girl Mickey had ever seen. But the prince! Br-r-r-rhh! Mickey shuddered. He had never seen anyone quite so ugly.

Princess Minnie had never seen the prince, and when she met him

there in front of the throne she paused, startled. He was more than homely; he was positively disgusting, she decided. And when he started to talk he only made things worse.

"I know you'll learn to love me!" he said.

Princess Minnie stopped and stamped her little foot.

"Never!" she cried. "Never, never, NEVER! I'd rather DIE!"

The King's eyes blazed with wrath. He stood up before his throne and pounded his scepter on the floor.

"What?" he bellowed. "You disobey me? All right. So be it. You have pronounced your own sentence. You will either marry the prince or you shall die!" He turned to two armed guards standing alongside him. "Lock her up in the tower!"

While Mickey watched, the guards dragged the poor little princess out of the room and started up the long, winding stairway that led to the tower.

"This is serious," Mickey said to himself as he jumped down from

his perch on the horse's head. "It looks as if it's up to me to get on the job and see if I can rescue her, or something."

As he walked around the corner of the building he saw the tower, a most forbidding structure, with a tiny window up near its top. Beside it was a tree.

Mickey wasted no time, but climbed the tree to the very top. When he saw the little princess' face in the window above, he began to sing:

"Cheer up, O lovely Princess,
For you'll be rescued soon.
I'll take thee away, so you won't have to stay
And marry that silly baboon!"

Mickey then jumped down to a lower branch which acted as a springboard and tossed him up to the window ledge. He hopped inside, doffed his hat, and bowed gracefully.

"Hello!" he said.

"Shhhhh——!" replied the princess, her finger on her lips.

"I'll save thee, Princess," he offered.

"But—but—but, how?" she asked.

"Hast thou a rope?"

"Nay, nay! No rope!"

"What? No rope?" Mickey looked across the room toward the bed. "Then we'll have to make one!"

Quickly he tied the bedclothes together, dangled them out the window, and tied one end to the bedstead. Then, with Princess Minnie under one arm, he started down the makeshift rope.

Unfortunately, he did not realize that the rope came down directly in front of the courtroom. And what was the king's surprise to look out the window and see his daughter and a strange minstrel sliding by.

"What ho! The guard!" he shouted. "The guard! The GUARD!" And before Mickey and Minnie knew what had happened, they were carried before the furious, thundering, storming king.

"Wretch! Scoundrel!" cried the king, pointing at Mickey. "Off with his cowardly head!"

"No! No!" screamed Minnie. "Not that, Father! At least, give him a chance for his life!"

"A chance? A chance?" The king hesitated. Then he roared with laughter. "All right," he shouted, "he shall have a chance. Let him fight a duel with the prince!"

The court took up the cry immediately and delightedly.

> "We're gonna have a duel!
> We're gonna have a duel!
> Heigh-ho, the Merry-o!
> We're gonna have a duel!"

This suited Mickey exactly. He had no fear of the gangling prince. He got his mule and rode to one end of the long hall, where there was a small stove. With a coal scuttle for a helmet, the stove for armor

and a curtain rod for a lance, he advanced to meet the prince, clad in full dueling regalia.

They came together in the center of the hall.

C-L-L-LANG! Both horse and mule went back on their haunches from the force of the collision. Neither rider was unseated, but Mickey's spear had broken against the prince's armor. Mickey was unarmed!

Springing from his mule's back, he dashed across the room to a guillotine standing in the corner. Jumping upon it, he turned and made a face at the prince, who had jumped from his horse and was chasing Mickey. Just as his spear was almost upon him, Mickey stepped aside and dropped the guillotine knife. The Prince's spear was cut in two, up close to the handle. Mickey grabbed it with a triumphant laugh. Now it was the prince who was unarmed.

The prince did not have Mickey's ability to make the best of a bad situation. He was terrified. He didn't know what Mickey was going to do, but he made up his mind that he would much rather be some place else when Mickey did it.

Around and around the room they went, with the prince howling and yowling at every step. He finally headed for a window, and made a flying leap through the glass, falling to the ground below and leaving Mickey the undisputed victor.

The castle fairly shook with the shouts and cheers of the knights and ladies who had watched the combat. They took Mickey and the little princess in their arms and carried them high over their heads to the front of the throne.

The King looked at them and smiled.

"Sir Mickey," he said, "you may not be a prince in name, but you are one in valor. As a reward for your heroism, you shall be given the hand of my daughter in wedlock." He looked at Princess Minnie and smiled again. "That is, if she is willing."

The little princess looked at Mickey. Then she blushed prettily and slipped her hand into his. She was willing.